Coral, Max & Chloe

D0576733

LOVE

Katrina & Ivan

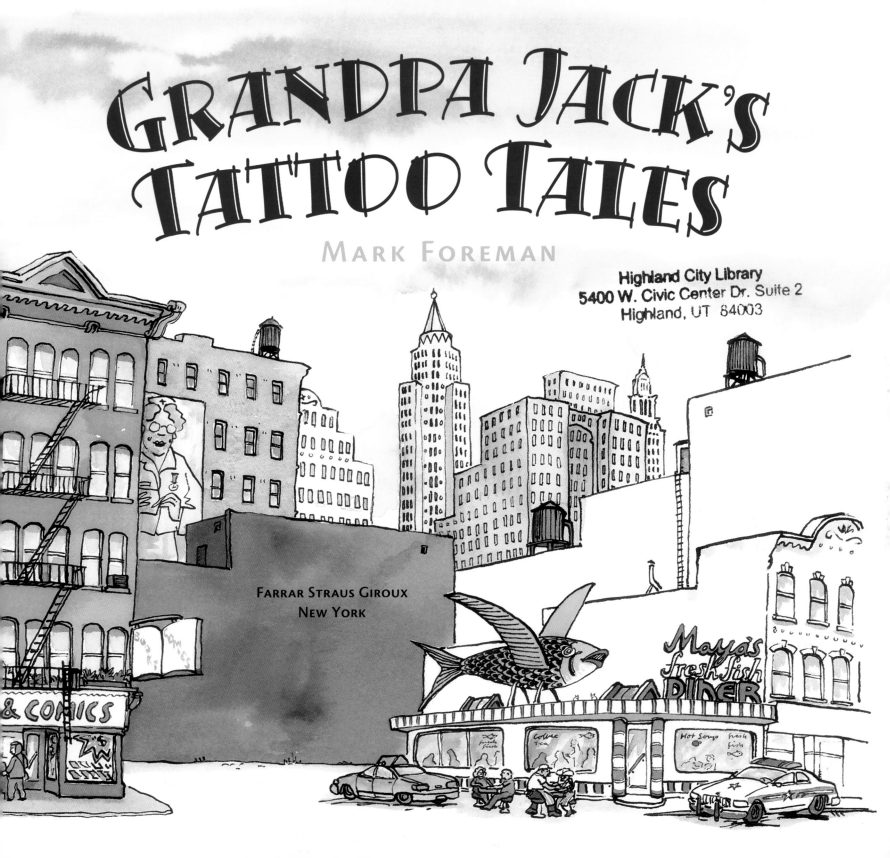

GRANDPA JACK'S TATTOO TALES

MARK FOREMAN

Farrar Straus Giroux
New York

For Caroline, Chloe, Sam, and all those at sea

Distributed in Canada by Douglas & McIntyre Ltd.
Color separations by Chroma Graphics PTE Ltd.
Printed and bound in China
Designed by Jay Colvin
First edition, 2007
1 3 5 7 9 10 8 6 4 2

www.fsgkidsbooks.com

Library of Congress Cataloging-in-Publication Data
Foreman, Mark.
   Grandpa Jack's tattoo tales / Mark Foreman.— 1st ed.
      p. cm.
   Summary: Chloe loves to spend time at her grandparents' restaurant, where she
gets to hear Grandpa Jack's stories about the many tattoos that commemorate events
in his life at sea.
   ISBN-13: 978-0-374-32768-2
   ISBN-10: 0-374-32768-8
   [1. Tattooing—Fiction.   2. Storytelling—Fiction.   3. Grandfathers—Fiction.
4. Sea stories.] I. Title.

PZ7.F75827 Gra 2007
[Fic]—dc22

2006040853

aya's Fresh Fish Diner was Chloe's favorite place to be. She usually
went to her grandparents' restaurant on days her mom was at work.
Grandpa Jack had a lot of tattoos, and he liked to tell all sorts of stories about them.
Sometimes they were stories Chloe knew, and other times they were ones she'd
never heard before. But no matter what, Chloe always loved his tattoo tales.

One afternoon, a family of tourists were paying their check when one of them asked Grandpa Jack, "Why do you have a tattoo of a rope?"
Chloe smiled because she knew what was coming next.

Grandpa Jack bellowed, "This is no ordinary rope! This lasso takes me back to when I was growing up down the street from here. I was a city kid through and through, but I loved Westerns. Cowboys were my heroes, and I sure wanted to be one. I practiced day and night with my trusty lasso.

"I thought my chance had come when I turned fourteen. I needed an after-school job, but nobody wanted a cowboy. Fortunately, I found other things to lasso when I started working down on the docks—boy, did I like tethering those boats!

"Most of the jobs were dirty and smelly, but I thought the wharf was exciting. As I got older, I moved on to bigger and dirtier boats.

"One day, while scrubbing a particularly filthy funnel, I saw an amazing sight. The fleet was in the bay. There were dozens of cruisers with colorful flags and smart sailors standing at attention on the gleaming decks.

"I was so thrilled by all of it that I decided to join the navy and see the world! Mind you, I didn't want to fight or touch the guns, so I was mighty relieved when I was ordered below deck.

"I was put to work with Ivan, the ship's cook. He and I became fast friends.

"I helped Ivan with the cooking and cleaning and we often went ashore for food. I also became an expert fisherman, catching fish of all shapes and sizes in every ocean of the world. Most of the day's catch went to the captain, who had a never-ending appetite.

"Shrimp, the ship's cat, sometimes managed to snag a fish.

"My mates cheered for me whenever I had a particularly good catch because it meant they would get fish for dinner, too.

"As time passed, I couldn't help but notice that nearly all my mates had colorful drawings on their arms. Some had beautiful pictures on their backs or their chests. I mentioned this to Ivan.

"'Ah, boy, you are not a real sailor until you have a tattoo!' he exclaimed. 'Tattoos remind us of all the wonderful things we've done in our lives. We will have to get you one.'

"In the next port of call, Ivan took me to the tattoo parlor. I didn't know what to get, so Ivan told me to start with a girlfriend's name.

"Well, I didn't have a girlfriend, so I chose my first cat's name instead. I didn't tell that to Ivan, though!

"Up until then, I'd never seen anything quite like that tattoo parlor. There were pictures of flags, flowers, animals, and people covering every wall. I have to admit my first tattoo hurt quite a bit. The others just made my skin tingle.

"Afterward I felt real proud of myself. But then Ivan showed me the tattoo on his back, and I felt like a fool. Mine was tiny.

"'Don't worry,' Ivan reassured me. 'I'm sure it will be the first of many.'

"As we traveled the world, I kept busy lassoing, fishing, and gathering fruit, vegetables, and tattoos. Life was going great, until I caught my biggest fish ever . . .

"But that humongous flying fish got clean away! And it took my little boat and my day's catch with it!

"The hungry captain was not pleased at all. He had been looking forward to a grand fish supper. As punishment, I was ordered to repaint the ship when we were next in port.

"I did, but I tinkered with the patterns and colors here and there.

"I thought the ship looked spiffy, and so did my mates. They even paid for a special tattoo to record the whole event.

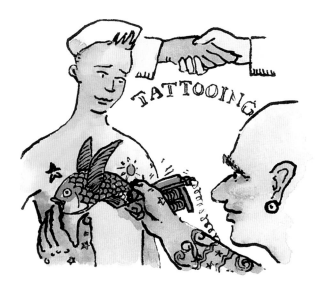

"However, the captain was not amused. He said I would be in a heap of trouble if I didn't put the ship back to normal. But I'd used up all the paint, so we set sail looking bright and pretty. Maybe too pretty . . .

"I don't know what attracted the octopus, but that beast took a liking to our ship.

"A cry went out: 'Abandon ship! Abandon ship!'

"My mates escaped together, but I couldn't leave without Shrimp. This began a new chapter in my life. We were on our own. Just Shrimp, me, my lasso, and a cooking pot.

"One night, there was a terrible storm . . .

"I lost my paddle, and we were stranded.

"But luck was on our side and we were rescued by a mermaid. As long as I live, I won't forget how that lovely lady brought us to dry land.

"Shrimp and I explored our new home. There was a white sandy beach with a dense jungle at its edge. I could fish and gather fruit.

"I tried going into the jungle, but it was far too dark! And I heard bloodcurdling animal noises coming from it at night.

"I built a tree house over the next few weeks. We could see for miles from our high-rise, but I never saw one passing ship.

"One day, I spotted smoke beyond the jungle. 'Civilization is out there,' I said to Shrimp. 'We must be brave and venture through that dreaded forest.'

"And so, trusty lasso at my side, we set off!

"At every step, there were all sorts of creatures and bugs that gave Shrimp and me a fright. But the deeper we went, the more courageous we became.

"I couldn't believe our good fortune when I spotted a tasty-looking snake. 'Snake steaks!' I cried. Quick as a flash, I lassoed that fellow. And I swear to you, that snake shot off, taking me with it. Poor Shrimp had to chase after us.

"I was dragged, bumped, and bashed, until I finally landed with a crash on a beach on the other side of the island.

"That's when, to my horror, I noticed I hadn't lassoed a delicious supper
but actually the tail of an enormous lizard.
"'This is it,' I said to Shrimp. 'We're lunch to this fellow!'

"'I see you've met Winston, my pet lizard,' said the most gorgeous woman I had ever seen. 'I think he likes you,' she added as this Winston critter slobbered all over me.

"The woman's name was Maya, and she lived on the island with her people. Their skin was covered with amazing pictures and patterns—far more than any of my navy mates had. Maya's people were great artists who believed their tattoos brought them luck. They admired my fish and my ship tattoos, though they didn't understand why I had 'Kitty' on my biceps.

"Over the following months, we all told stories. As I told them my adventures, they illustrated them on my arms, my back, and a few other places.

"Maya and I fell in love and got married.
When we had a baby girl, we called her Coral.
I was one happy man, but a part of me missed
the noise and commotion of the city.

"One fateful day, I spotted a small dinghy approaching the island. And then a large man came bounding up the beach toward me. It was Ivan! I couldn't believe my eyes.

"'I haven't stopped looking for you since the shipwreck!' cried Ivan. 'I've checked every island I've come across. I knew I'd find you.'

"Shrimp was very excited to see Ivan again, too.

"After a few days of catching up, we all decided to head off to my old hometown and set up a little business of our own.

"Ivan, Maya, and I opened this diner, and here we are today, still cooking and still fishing together after all these years."

Grandpa Jack finished his story. The tourists all looked amazed.

One of them pointed at a bandage on Jack's arm and asked, "Is that a new tattoo? What's that one?"

"I bet it's a lion or a pirate ship," another said.

Grandpa Jack chuckled and said, "No, it's even more extraordinary."

Jack, Maya, and Coral

Shrimp and family